Dear Fam[...]

What'[...] child love reading:

Find good books like this one to share—and read together!

Here are some tips.

●**Take a "picture walk."** Look at all the pictures before you read. Talk about what you see.

●**Take turns.** Read to your child. Ham it up! Use different voices for different characters, and read with feeling! Then listen as your child reads to you, or explains the story in his or her own words.

●**Point out words as you read.** Help your child notice how letters and sounds go together. Point out unusual or difficult words that your child might not know. Talk about those words and what they mean.

●**Ask questions.** Stop to ask questions as you read. For example: "What do you think will happen next?" "How would you feel if that happened to you?"

●**Read every day.** Good stories are worth reading more than once! Read signs, labels, and even cereal boxes with your child. Visit the library to take out more books. And look for other JUST FOR YOU! BOOKS you and your child can share!

The Editors

For the beautiful souls of my children
—IS

For Tomie dePaola, who sparked my imagination
—AB

Text copyright © 2003 by Irene Smalls.
Illustrations copyright © 2003 by Aaron Boyd.
Produced for Scholastic by COLOR-BRIDGE BOOKS, LLC, Brooklyn, NY
All rights reserved. Published by SCHOLASTIC INC.
JUST FOR YOU! is a trademark of Scholastic Inc.

ISBN 0-439-56852-8

10 9 8 7 6   05 06 07

23

Printed in the U.S.A.
First Scholastic Printing, December 2003

I CAN'T TAKE A BATH!

by Irene Smalls
Illustrated by Aaron Boyd

JUST FOR YOU!™ Level 2

I can't take a bath, Mom!
Can't you give me a break?
I've got this really bad, awful headache.
I think a bath would be a big mistake.

The thing about baths,
Mom, is they never last.
Next thing I know, you'll want me
to take another one.

We have to save water!
Think of the thirsty plants,
the dying fish!

I want to save them.
That's my wish!

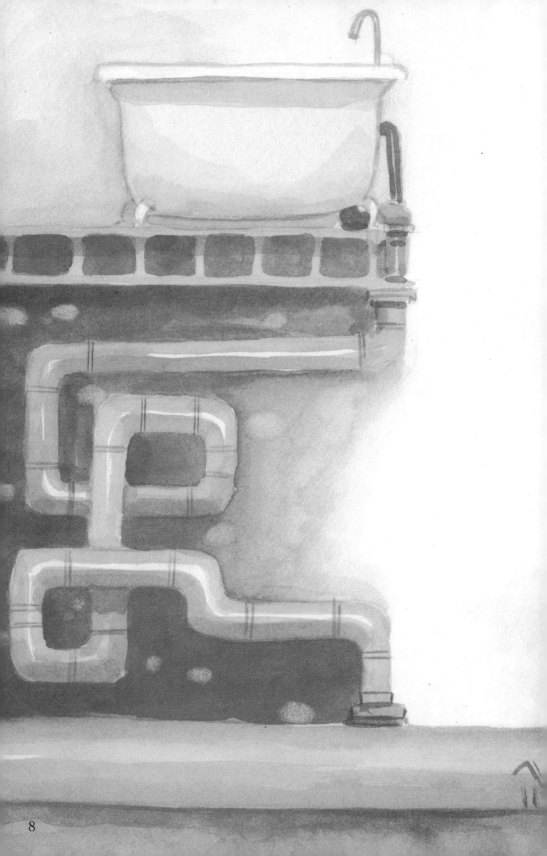

There's this boy I know
who took a bath. . . .
He's never been heard from again!
I can't take that path.
It makes me sad just to
think about him!

Oh, Mom, I forgot!
There's a monster in the bathroom!
Going in there would mean certain doom.
He's been to every house on our street.

Now it's our turn.
He makes your skin itch,
your hair fall out,
and your ears burn!

Hmmm, I see. . . .
No monster under there.

Well, I think you gave him
quite a scare.

Uh-oh, Mom, I'm going to sneeze.
You don't want me to catch some terrible disease!

Oh, no, I feel sick.
I need to go to bed.
You really want me to take a bath instead?

Okay, okay.
Close your eyes.
No peeking!
Don't look now!
No fair sneaking!

Turn your back.
Step outside.
Now close the door.

Hear that water splashing?
Hear those boats crashing?

I'm taking a great bath!

Okay, okay!
I'll get in the water this time.
Taking a bath should be a crime!

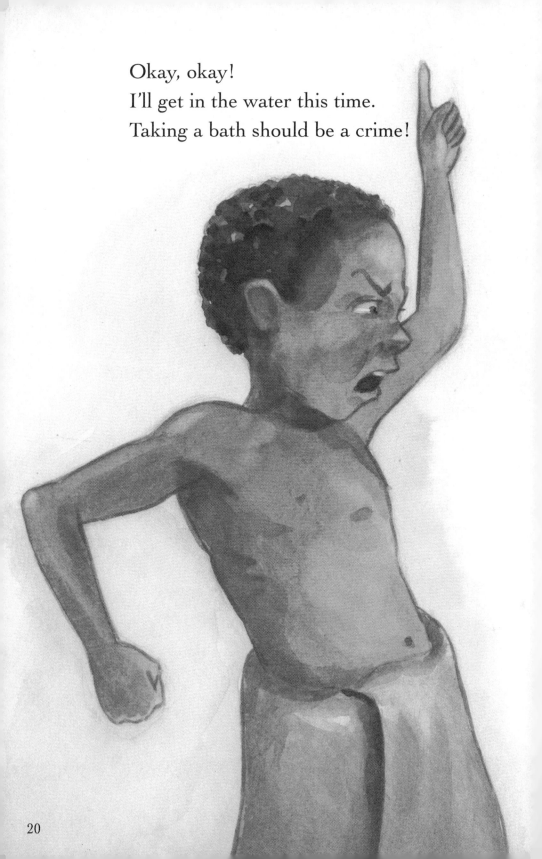

But wait, Mom!
I don't have the right soap.
I can't take a bath without
my soap on a rope!

I need my special towel, too.
No, not the red one!
My towel is blue.

I also need my rubber ducky.
Taking a bath is just so yucky!

I know this water must be too hot. . . .

Oh, no, it's not!

Okay, okay, I guess it's not so bad.
Please close the shower curtain just a tad.

Mom, I'm a sea serpent.
From the deep sea I was sent. . . .

Now I'm a submarine,
so far underwater I can't be seen.

Ooooh! This bath is so nice. . . .
Mom, can I take a bath twice?

▲▲▲▲▲ JUST FOR YOU ▲▲▲▲▲

Here are some fun things for you to do.

YOUR Time to Rhyme

The author had fun writing
the rhymes for this story.

What word did she use to rhyme
with fish? ▲
What else rhymes with fish?

Can you make up your own rhyme
with words that rhyme with fish?

What word did she use
to rhyme with bed? ▲

What else rhymes with bed?

What other fun rhymes can
you find in this book?

▲ wish   ▲ instead

The Monster and YOU!

Aaron Boyd drew the pictures for this book. He made the monster big, green, and very silly!

YOU can draw a silly monster, too.

Think about what your monster will look like. What would it do if it saw you? What would you do if you saw it?

Now draw yourself with your monster. Show your picture to your friends.

▲▲▲▲TOGETHER TIME ▲▲▲▲

Make some time to share ideas about the story with your young reader! Here are some activities you can try. There are no right or wrong answers.

Think About It: Ask your child, "Why do you think the boy's mother wants him to take a bath? Why do you think the boy finally changed his mind about taking a bath?"

Read It Again: Read the story aloud to your child, with a hip-hop beat! You can both move to the beat as you read.

Talk About It: Part of what makes this story so much fun to read is its blend of the real and the make-believe. Ask your child, "Which things in the story could really happen? Which things could NEVER happen in real life?"

Meet the Author

IRENE SMALLS says, "I wrote *I Can't Take a Bath!* because I knew a little boy who hated to take baths. We would play games to get him into the bathtub and sometimes we sang songs about taking baths. We would even take turns taking a bath! After he got into the tub, he liked it. But I always had a hard time getting him to take a bath."

Irene is a storyteller, author, and historian. She grew up in Harlem, New York, received her Master's Degree from New York University, and now lives in Boston, Massachusetts. She writes children's books because she has a little girl inside her who never grew up. Many of her stories are about that little girl's feelings, thoughts, and adventures. Irene fell in love with reading when she was in Kindergarten. Her teacher would read stories with great expression, sound effects, and accents. Irene was excited by the music her teacher made when reading words on a page out loud.

Meet the Artist

AARON BOYD says, "When I was six years old, I knew that I wanted to illustrate children's books. That's when I read *Strega Nona*, by Tomie dePaola. I took that book out of my school library every week. I copied the pictures until I could draw the whole book from memory! I really enjoyed working on *I Can't Take a Bath!* It reminded me of the books that I liked to read when I was a kid. It is funny, colorful, and true. But I have to admit, I do like to take baths now!"

Aaron has been an illustrator for more than ten years. He likes to draw stories about animals, and he especially likes to work on books with multicultural themes. Aaron thinks it is important for stories to reflect all the different kinds of people around us. He lives in Milwaukee, Wisconsin, with his best friend, his dog Queen.